Dear Parent:
Your child's love of re

Every child learns to read in a different way and at his or her own speed. Some go back and forth between reading levels and read favorite books again and again. Others read through each level in order. You can help your young reader improve and become more confident by encouraging his or her own interests and abilities. From books your child reads with you to the first books he or she reads alone, there are I Can Read Books for every stage of reading:

SHARED READING
Basic language, word repetition, and whimsical illustrations, ideal for sharing with your emergent reader

BEGINNING READING
Short sentences, familiar words, and simple concepts for children eager to read on their own

READING WITH HELP
Engaging stories, longer sentences, and language play for developing readers

READING ALONE
Complex plots, challenging vocabulary, and high-interest topics for the independent reader

ADVANCED READING
Short paragraphs, chapters, and exciting themes for the perfect bridge to chapter books

I Can Read Books have introduced children to the joy of reading since 1957. Featuring award-winning authors and illustrators and a fabulous cast of beloved characters, I Can Read Books set the standard for beginning readers.

A lifetime of discovery begins with the magical words **"I Can Read!"**

Visit www.icanread.com for information
on enriching your child's reading experience.

For kindhearted Kristen Shaleen,
foster mom to cats
—J.H.

For those who keep us safe
—J.B.

I Can Read Book® is a trademark of HarperCollins Publishers.

Itty Bitty Kitty: Firehouse Fun
Copyright © 2016 by HarperCollins Publishers
All rights reserved. Manufactured in U.S.A.
No part of this book may be used or reproduced in any manner whatsoever without written permission except in the case of brief quotations embodied in critical articles and reviews. For information address HarperCollins Children's Books, a division of HarperCollins Publishers, 195 Broadway, New York, NY 10007.
www.icanread.com

Library of Congress Control Number: 2015947481
ISBN 978-0-06-232222-7 (trade bdg.) — ISBN 978-0-06-232221-0 (pbk.)

17 18 19 20 LSCC 10 9 8 7 6 5 4 3 ❖ First Edition

ITTY BITTY KITTY

FIREHOUSE FUN

ITTY BITTY

I.B.K.

KITTY

by Joan Holub

illustrated by James Burks

HARPER

An Imprint of HarperCollinsPublishers

It is a big day
at the firehouse.
Ava goes to visit.

So does her cat.

His name is Itty Bitty.

But he is not itty. Or bitty.

There are snacks for all
in the firehouse.
Ava gets a little snack.

Itty Bitty gets a little snack.
And another. And another.
Ah, just right.

Look!

Ava sees something wiggle.

What could it be?

A fire hose!
Firefighter Smitty
shows Ava how to spray water.

Water is an itty bitty bit
too wet for a cat.

Now Itty Bitty sees
something wiggle!

What could it be?

It is a tail!
A tail that belongs
to a firehouse dog.

"MEOW," says Itty Bitty.

"GRR," says the firehouse dog.

The firehouse dog runs away.
Does he want to play chase?

Itty Bitty likes this game.
The firehouse dog
does not like it.
Not one itty bitty bit!

Off they go!
Itty Bitty runs past
hats, coats, and boots.

Where is that firehouse dog?

Is he up here?

Is he down there?

Itty Bitty goes down.

Itty Bitty gets stuck!

Oh, Itty Bitty.

"You are too big," says Ava.

Itty Bitty does not think
he is too big.
He thinks the hole
is too small.

Hey! There's that dog again!

It zooms away.

Itty Bitty zooms after it.

Oops!

They bump a button.

RRR-RRR

CRASH!

The firefighters hear the alarm.

They run over.

But there is not a real fire.

RRRRRRRR~

RRRRR!!

The firehouse dog howls.

Itty Bitty howls.

"Oh, Itty Bitty," says Ava.

Now Firefighter Smitty
shows them how to stay safe
if there is a real fire.

"When smoke goes UP,
you go DOWN,"
Firefighter Smitty tells them.

Itty Bitty
and the firehouse dog
learn to be safe, too.

IF YOUR CLOTHES CATCH FIRE:

 **STOP**

 **DROP**

AND

 **ROLL**

Itty Bitty and the dog stop,

drop,

and roll.

Now Ava and Itty Bitty
say good-bye.
Ava made a new friend today.

Itty Bitty made
a new friend, too.

Itty Bitty, what a kitty!